Shadows
A War of Faith
By Jayne Adriel

This is a work of fiction. Names, characters, places, and incidents are the product of the author's imagination or are used fictitiously. Any resemblance to actual events, locales, or persons, living or dead, is entirely coincidental.

To all the dreamers, believers, and seekers,

This book is dedicated to you. In the midst of life's uncertainties and shadows, may the journey of Aria Everwood inspire you to embrace your own unique path, fueled by unwavering faith and a resilient spirit. Just as Aria's story unfolds from doubt to divine purpose, may you find solace and strength in your journey.

"For we walk by faith, not by sight."
2 Corinthians 5:7

May these words resonate within you, guiding you through the challenges and victories that life brings. Remember, you are never alone. Let the light of faith illuminate your path and lead you from shadows to the brilliance of purpose.

With love,

Jayne Adriel

Table Of Contents

7 Chapter 1: Meet Aria

11 Chapter 2: Lily's Absence

19 Chapter 3: Aria's Emotional Struggles

27 Chapter 4: The Hidden World

34 Chapter 5: Temptation and Struggle

42 Chapter 6: Persistent Prayer

49 Chapter 7: The Warrior

61 Chapter 8: From Shadows to Light

69 Epilogue

CHAPTER 1

Meet Aria

A teenage girl named Aria Everwood lived in a quiet town where laughter echoed through the streets, and dreams floated like whispers in the air. With sun-kissed hair that framed her delicate face and eyes that sparkled with curiosity, she was a canvas of vibrant emotions waiting to be painted with life's experiences.

Aria's days were woven with the threads of high school routines, where classrooms transformed into landscapes of learning and friendships were nurtured like fragile blooms. She navigated the hallways with a quiet grace, her presence a blend of introspection and warm kindness that drew people to her. There was an air of mystery about Aria, an aura that spoke of secrets held close, yet a heart open to connection.

Dancing and painting were the colors that painted her life's canvas. When the last bell of the school day rang, Aria's heart quickened in anticipation. It was her time, a sacred moment when she could let her spirit soar. Whether it was the graceful sway of her body or the strokes of her brush on canvas, Aria found solace in the rhythmic cadence of movement and color. She would lose herself in the dance studio, her body expressing emotions too complex for words. And when she held a paintbrush, her thoughts would dance onto the canvas, creating a symphony of hues that spoke of her inner world.

But beneath her vibrant exterior lay a history of pain that shaped her in ways unseen. Aria's parents had parted ways when she was just five years old, leaving a void in her heart that she had struggled to fill. Her father had stepped away, starting a new family, and though her mother's love was unwavering, Aria felt the ache of abandonment like a haunting melody. Her father's absence was a puzzle with missing pieces, and Aria had pieced together her own narrative of what had gone wrong.

Her mother, a woman of strength and grace, had tried to fill the void with love and stories of a God who had become Aria's Father in a way her earthly father never had. "God is your Father now," her mother would say, her voice gentle and soothing. But as Aria watched her friends share moments with their fathers, a pang of longing would tug at her heart, a reminder of the empty space that no one else could truly fill.

Amidst this emotional landscape, Aria found a beacon of light named Lily. Their friendship had been forged in a dance class when they were just eight years old, a bond formed by shared giggles and synchronized dance steps. Lily's laughter was like a melody that danced in harmony with Aria's heart, and their connection grew deeper with each passing day.

Lily was a whirlwind of energy, her enthusiasm infectious and her spirit unyielding. Together, Aria and Lily navigated the labyrinth of childhood and adolescence, two souls intertwined in a friendship that was as natural as breathing.

They would spend hours in Aria's room, sharing secrets, dreams, and fears. When one was down, the other would be there with a smile or a comforting presence, a testament to the kind of friendship that is forged in the crucible of life's challenges.

The memory of the day they met was etched in Aria's mind like a snapshot from a treasured album. They had stood side by side, two young girls with dreams in their eyes and uncertainty in their hearts. As the dance instructor clapped their hands to signal the start of the music, Aria and Lily had exchanged a nervous smile. And in that moment, their souls had connected in a way that needed no words.

Aria's heart resonated with gratitude for the friendship that had become her anchor through life's storms. Lily was the one who had seen her through every trial, every triumph, and every tear. Their bond was unbreakable, a lifeline that had pulled Aria from the depths of despair and into the light of acceptance and love.

In the midst of her love for dancing, painting, and the comfort of her friendship with Lily, Aria's heart held a yearning—a yearning to understand her own worth, her own identity. The pain of her father's absence lingered like a shadow, casting doubt on her value. And as Aria stood at the crossroads of adolescence, she found herself grappling with questions that seemed to echo in the chambers of her soul: Was she worthy of love? Was she truly seen and known?

As Aria stepped into each new day, she was unaware of the journey that lay ahead—a journey that would lead her from the shadows of her past to the brilliant light of a faith that could mend even the deepest of wounds. The dance of life had twists and turns she couldn't predict, but her heart beat with a hope that there was something more waiting to unfold—a tapestry of moments, friendships, and encounters that would shape her into the woman she was destined to become.

CHAPTER 2

Lily's Absence

Aria had spent months preparing for the dance concert, pouring her heart and soul into every practice session. The dance routine had become more than just movements; it was an expression of her emotions, a testament to her dedication and passion. As the day of the concert approached, Aria's excitement mixed with nervous anticipation. She knew that this performance was a culmination of hard work, a chance to prove to herself and the world that she could shine.

Backstage, Aria adjusted her costume one last time, her heart racing in time with the rhythm of the music playing in the auditorium. The dim glow of the stage lights filtered through the heavy curtain, casting long shadows on the floor. Her breath came in shallow bursts as she mentally went over every step, every move. This was her moment.

When the stage manager announced her name, Aria took a deep breath and stepped into the spotlight. The bright lights blinded her momentarily, but as the music began to play, her focus narrowed to the dance floor. With each step, each leap, she poured her emotions into the performance, letting the music guide her body like a brush on a canvas.

As the final notes of the music echoed through the auditorium, Aria struck her closing pose with a flourish. The audience erupted into applause, a sea of faces blending into a blur of appreciation. Her heart swelled with a sense of accomplishment, a feeling of triumph that she had conquered the stage, even if just for a few minutes.

After the concert, as Aria basked in the glow of her success, she eagerly scanned the crowd for Lily's familiar face. They had attended every significant event in each other's lives, and Aria expected her best friend to be there to share in this moment. However, as the minutes turned into a quarter of an hour, Aria's excitement began to wane. A sinking feeling settled in the pit of her stomach.

As the cheers of the audience faded into the background, Aria found herself questioning Lily's absence. The bond they shared was unbreakable, and Lily had never missed any of Aria's performances. Confusion and hurt intertwined within Aria's thoughts as she struggled to understand why her best friend wasn't there to support her.

Returning home after the concert, Aria's phone sat silent on her desk. She checked it repeatedly, hoping for a message from Lily explaining her absence, but the screen remained empty. Aria's heart felt heavy, a mix of disappointment and worry gnawing at her. She replayed their conversations in her mind, searching for clues or hints that she might have missed. Why had Lily not shown up? What could have caused her best friend to suddenly withdraw without any explanation?

In the days that followed, Aria's hurt grew deeper. Her mom had thrown a small celebration to commemorate her achievement, inviting close friends and family. Aria had hoped that Lily would make a surprise appearance, that the absence at the concert would be explained with a burst of laughter and a warm hug. But as the hours ticked by, it became clear that Lily wasn't coming.

Aria watched the door, her heart sinking with each passing moment. She felt a pang of loneliness as she looked around at the people gathered to celebrate her success. It wasn't the same without Lily by her side, without her partner in crime to share in the joy and pride.

As the celebration continued without Lily, Aria's confusion turned to a deeper sense of hurt. She couldn't understand why her best friend had disappeared without a word, leaving her to navigate the aftermath of her triumph alone. The questions and doubts swirled in her mind, casting shadows over what should have been a moment of pure happiness.

Amid the laughter and chatter of the party, Aria's heartache was a silent ache that couldn't be ignored. Lily's absence had left a void that seemed to echo the absence she had felt ever since her dad had left. In that moment, surrounded by the people who loved her, Aria couldn't shake the feeling of being abandoned once again.

The days that followed the concert were marked by a heavy cloud of uncertainty for Aria. The hurt from Lily's absence lingered, a constant reminder that something was amiss. Aria had always thought that no matter what happened, she and Lily would face it together. Their friendship was the cornerstone of her life, an unbreakable bond that had weathered every storm.

Aria's fingers hovered over her phone as she debated whether to reach out to Lily. She scrolled through their past messages, trying to find any sign of a missed communication, a misunderstanding. But the conversations were the same as she remembered—filled with laughter, shared excitement, and plans for the concert. There was no indication that something had gone wrong between them.

Over time, Aria couldn't shake the feeling of confusion and hurt. The silence from Lily was deafening, an unspoken void that grew with each passing moment. Aria's phone stayed silent, devoid of the messages and calls that used to be a constant presence. She missed the late-night conversations, the random memes, and the heart-to-heart talks that had woven their lives together.

One evening, as Aria scrolled through her Instagram feed, her heart plummeted. There, amidst a cascade of images, was Lily. She was posing with a group of friends, their smiles wide and their camaraderie evident. Aria's breath caught in her throat as she looked closer, recognizing the faces of people she had seen at the party her mom had thrown. Lily was out with them, enjoying herself as if nothing had changed.

The hurt that had been simmering beneath the surface erupted into a whirlwind of emotions. Betrayal, confusion, and anger churned within Aria's chest. How could Lily be out with other friends, smiling and laughing, while she was left in the dark? The images on the screen felt like a slap in the face, a painful reminder that Lily had seemingly moved on without her.

Aria's fingers trembled as she typed out a message to Lily, her words a mix of frustration and hurt. She asked why Lily hadn't been there for her, why she had chosen to distance herself when Aria needed her the most. The minutes stretched into what felt like an eternity as Aria waited for a response. Her heart raced, her mind spiraling with thoughts of what Lily's explanation might be.

When the response finally came, it was short and lacked the warmth that had once been a hallmark of their friendship. Lily's words were measured, almost detached, as if she were talking to a distant acquaintance rather than her best friend. She explained that she had been busy with other commitments and hadn't been able to make it to the concert or the celebration.

Aria's heart sank further. The words felt like a hollow excuse, a flimsy attempt to explain away the hurt she had caused. She had thought that Lily would be there to share in her triumph, to stand by her side like she always had. The realization that Lily had chosen not to be there, that she had prioritized other friends over their bond, was a painful blow that cut deep.

Tears welled in Aria's eyes as she read and reread Lily's message. She had believed in their friendship so strongly, had trusted that Lily would never let her down. The disconnect between her expectations and the reality before her was a stark reminder that people could change, that even the strongest bonds could be tested.

In the days that followed, Aria grappled with a mix of emotions. Anger battled with sadness, confusion wrestled with a deep sense of loss. She found herself questioning everything —their shared memories, their late-night talks, the promises they had made to each other. It was as if the foundation of her world had been shaken, leaving her adrift in a sea of uncertainty.

Every time Aria saw another post on Lily's social media, the wound was freshly salted. Images of her best friend having fun with other people were a stark contrast to the emptiness Aria felt. The hurt had burrowed deep within her heart, and every glance at her phone seemed to twist the knife a little further.

Aria's mom noticed the change in her daughter, the way her smile didn't reach her eyes, the moments of silence that lingered between them. Aria tried to brush off her concerns, but her mom saw through the facade. One evening, as they sat on the porch watching the sunset, Aria's mom gently asked about Lily.

Tears filled Aria's eyes as she shared the story—the concert, Lily's absence, the images on Instagram. Her mom listened attentively, her presence a comfort for Aria's wounded heart.

When she spoke, her words were filled with understanding and wisdom, a reminder that friendships could face challenges but could also emerge stronger from them.

"Aria," her mom said, her voice soft yet firm, "Friendships, like any relationship, can go through ups and downs. People change, and sometimes they make choices that hurt us. But true friendships, the ones that are meant to be, find a way to heal. Maybe there's a misunderstanding, maybe Lily is going through something you don't know about. The important thing is to communicate, to express how you feel."

Aria's mom's words resonated within her, a gentle reminder that the foundation of their friendship was worth fighting for. With a determined spark in her eyes, Aria realized that she couldn't let their bond crumble without a fight. She deserved answers, and Lily deserved a chance to explain.

With a deep breath, Aria typed out a message to Lily, her words a careful blend of vulnerability and honesty. She let Lily know how hurt she was, how confused and abandoned she felt. She shared the memories they had created, the promises they had made, and the pain she was experiencing because of their current situation.

The response was slower this time, as if Lily was carefully choosing her words. When the message finally came, Aria's heart skipped a beat. Lily admitted that she had been avoiding Aria, that she had been intentionally ignoring her messages and calls. She didn't offer much explanation, only that she thought it was best for both of them.

Aria's hands trembled as she read those words, a mixture of shock and disbelief washing over her. How could Lily just ignore her, cut her out of her life without a valid reason? The pain intensified as Aria realized that their friendship, the bond she had cherished so dearly, was unraveling before her eyes.

Tears streamed down Aria's face as she absorbed the reality of Lily's words. The hurt was almost too much to bear, a heavy weight pressing down on her chest. She had trusted Lily with her heart, had believed that their friendship was unbreakable. The abruptness of Lily's abandonment left Aria feeling wounded and lost.

In the midst of her anguish, Aria's mom remained a steadfast pillar of support. She held Aria as she cried, her embrace a safe haven in the storm of emotions. "Sweetheart," her mom whispered, her voice soft and comforting, "Sometimes people make choices that we can't understand. It's not a reflection of your worth, but rather a reflection of their own struggles. It's okay to feel hurt, but remember that you are strong and resilient. This pain will pass, and you'll emerge even stronger."

CHAPTER 3

Aria's Emotional Struggles

Aria's world had been turned upside down. The hurt from Lily's abandonment echoed in the empty spaces of her heart, mirroring the pain she had felt when her father had walked out on her family. It was a familiar ache, a feeling of being left behind, of not being enough to keep those she loved close.

As she navigated her days, the absence of Lily seemed to cast a shadow over everything. The places they had once visited together felt different, the memories tainted by the knowledge that Lily was no longer a part of her life. Aria found herself reliving moments from the past, the times when her dad had been there to share in her joys and sorrows. It was as if history was repeating itself, as if the people she loved were destined to leave her behind.

Aria's art, once a source of solace, now felt like a reminder of her pain. She stared at the canvas, the brush poised in her hand, but the inspiration that had always flowed effortlessly seemed to have dried up. The vibrant colors were replaced by a muted palette that reflected the turmoil within her. She couldn't escape the feeling that she was losing herself, that the hurt was consuming every aspect of her life.

In the quiet moments of the night, when the world was still and the only sound was the rhythm of her own heartbeat, Aria's thoughts turned to God. Her mom had always told her that God was her father now, that He loved her unconditionally. But as Aria lay in bed, her heart heavy with the weight of her pain, she found herself questioning that love. If God truly loved her, why had He allowed the people she cared about to abandon her?

Aria's fingers traced the worn pages of her Bible, searching for answers. She opened to a passage that her mom had shared with her in times of difficulty, a verse that had brought comfort and reassurance. "The Lord is close to the brokenhearted and saves those who are crushed in spirit." (Psalm 34:18, NIV)

The words were a lifeline in the midst of her emotional turmoil. Aria clung to them, repeating them like a mantra as tears streamed down her face. She yearned to feel God's presence, to believe that He was indeed close to her, that He saw the pain in her heart.

But the questions persisted. How could she reconcile the idea of God's love with the hurt she was experiencing? How could she trust in a love that seemed so fragile, so prone to abandonment? Aria's faith was shaken, her once unshakable trust in God's goodness now faltering under the weight of her pain.

One evening, as Aria sat by her window, gazing at the stars, she whispered a prayer into the quiet night. "God, if you're there, if you truly love me, why does it feel like everyone I care about leaves? Why does it feel like I'm always left behind?"

The stars glittered in response, but the silence felt deafening. Aria's heart ached for a sign, for a sense of assurance that God was listening, that He cared about her pain. She longed for the kind of comfort she had found in her father's arms when she was a child, the feeling of being held and protected.

Weeks passed, and Aria's emotional struggle continued. She wrestled with her doubts, her faith, and the pain that seemed to have taken up residence in her heart. She tried to immerse herself in her art, in the familiar strokes of the brush against canvas, hoping that it would bring her some measure of relief.

One afternoon, as Aria was organizing her art supplies, she came across an old journal. It was a gift from her dad, something he had given her before he had left. She opened its pages, her fingers brushing against the words he had written. "My dear Aria, you are a masterpiece, a creation of love and beauty. No matter where life takes you, always remember that you are cherished."

Tears welled in Aria's eyes as she read those words. It was as if her dad was speaking to her across time, reminding her of his love and the love that had always been a part of her life. Aria realized that while people might leave, their love could continue to shape and guide her.

With a renewed determination, Aria returned to her Bible. She sought out passages that spoke of God's unwavering love, His faithfulness even in the face of pain and uncertainty. She found comfort in verses like Jeremiah 29:11: "'For I know the plans I have for you,' declares the Lord, 'plans to prosper you and not to harm you, plans to give you hope and a future.'" (NIV)

Slowly, Aria's heart began to open up to the possibility that God's love was different from the human love she had experienced. It was a love that transcended circumstances, a love that was constant even when people faltered. She realized that just as her dad had cherished her, God cherished her even more deeply.

In the midst of her struggles, Aria began to pray with a newfound honesty. She poured out her doubts, her pain, and her questions before God, trusting that He was listening. She asked for the strength to believe in His love, even when life felt uncertain and painful.

As Aria continued to seek solace in her faith, she found a glimmer of hope amidst the darkness. The emotional turmoil didn't vanish overnight, but it slowly began to lessen its grip on her heart. The pain was still there, but it was no longer suffocating.

Aria learned that faith wasn't about having all the answers, but about embracing the mystery and trusting in the One who held the universe in His hands. She realized that her journey was a process, a weaving together of her pain and her faith, forming a tapestry of resilience and growth.

With time, Aria's heart began to heal. The wounds of abandonment were still a part of her story, but they no longer defined her. She discovered that God's love was a constant presence, a source of strength that carried her through the darkest of times.

In the quiet moments of reflection, Aria found herself returning to the words her dad had written in her journal. "You are a masterpiece." Those words held a new meaning now. She was a masterpiece, not because of the love she received from others, but because of the love that resided within her and the love that enveloped her from above.

Aria's journey from pain to healing was far from over, but as she looked back on her struggles, she realized that her faith had grown stronger. The doubts and questions had given way to a deeper understanding of God's love—a love that was unwavering, unbreakable, and always there to guide her from shadows to light.

Late one night, with the soft glow of her laptop casting a gentle light across her room, Aria delved into the world of online resources. She typed in keywords like "handling pain," "forgiveness," and "finding joy amid sorrow." Page after page of articles, blog posts, and videos appeared, each promising insight into the struggles she was facing.

Aria clicked on a video that resonated with her—the speaker's calm voice and empathetic words drew her in. The video was about the power of forgiveness, how releasing the grip of anger and resentment could lead to healing. As Aria listened, she thought about Lily and the hurt she had caused. She realized that forgiveness wasn't about excusing Lily's actions, but about freeing herself from the weight of bitterness.

After the video ended, Aria found herself lost in thought. Forgiveness was a concept she had heard about before, but putting it into practice felt like an insurmountable challenge. Could she really let go of the hurt Lily had caused? Could she find it within herself to forgive, even when the pain felt so raw?

Aria's exploration led her to an article that discussed finding joy in the midst of pain. The author shared personal experiences and practical tips for cultivating gratitude and positivity, even when life seemed overwhelmingly difficult. Aria realized that joy wasn't about denying her pain, but about acknowledging it while also embracing the moments of beauty and goodness that still existed.

In her quest for answers, Aria's attention turned to the Bible. She had grown up hearing stories of faith, of people who had faced trials and emerged stronger because of their trust in God. She wanted to understand God's nature better, to comprehend His role as a father in her life. Could He truly be the father that her own dad had never been?

Aria began to read the Bible with fresh eyes, seeking out passages that spoke of God's love and His faithfulness. She stumbled upon a verse that resonated deeply within her heart: "The Lord is compassionate and gracious, slow to anger, abounding in love." (Psalm 103:8, NIV)

As she pondered those words, Aria felt a sense of comfort wash over her. The image of a compassionate and loving God began to take shape in her mind—a God who understood her pain, who cared about the depths of her heartache. She realized that God's love wasn't fickle, like the love she had experienced from humans; it was unwavering and unchanging.

Aria's Bible reading also led her to verses that spoke of God's role as a father. She read about how God cared for His children, how He provided, protected, and guided them. Aria saw parallels between these descriptions and the role her dad had once played in her life—the fatherly love that had always been a part of her identity.

With each page she turned, Aria felt a growing sense of connection with God. She saw the beauty of His love, the way it differed from human love but was no less powerful. As she navigated the passages of the Bible, Aria began to see that God's love was a love that would never abandon or betray her, a love that would always be her anchor.

In the quiet moments of contemplation, Aria found herself praying with a new understanding. She opened her heart to God, sharing her pain, doubts, and fears. She asked for the strength to forgive Lily, to release the bitterness that had taken root within her. She asked for the ability to find joy, even in the midst of her sorrow.

With each prayer, Aria felt a sense of peace enveloping her, a reassurance that she wasn't alone in her struggles. The wounds of abandonment were still there, but they were no longer defining her. Aria was learning to see herself through the lens of God's love—a love that had the power to heal, to transform, and to bring light to even the darkest corners of her heart.

As she closed her Bible one evening, Aria felt a profound sense of gratitude.

CHAPTER 4

The Hidden World

Aria's life had been a journey of pain, healing, and rediscovery. Just as she began to find her footing again, a new chapter of her story unfolded—one that would take her beyond the boundaries of her known world and into the realm of the extraordinary.

It all started with an ordinary afternoon. Aria was cleaning out the attic, sifting through old boxes of memories and forgotten treasures. Amidst the dust and cobwebs, her fingers brushed against something smooth and cold. She pulled out an intricately carved wooden box, its surface etched with patterns that seemed to tell a story.

Curiosity piqued, Aria opened the box, revealing an ancient-looking artifact nestled within. It was a pendant, held by a delicate chain, that gleamed with an otherworldly light. The pendant was adorned with symbols that Aria couldn't recognize, symbols that seemed to shimmer and dance as if alive.

As she held the pendant in her hand, Aria felt a tingling sensation, a sensation that seemed to resonate deep within her.

It was as if the pendant held a secret, a hidden truth that was waiting to be uncovered. Aria's heart raced as she considered the possibility that this artifact held a power beyond her understanding.

Yet skepticism was quick to follow. Aria had always been a practical person, someone who relied on logic and reason. The idea of a hidden world of angels and demons seemed far-fetched, the stuff of fairy tales and mythology. Could this pendant truly be a gateway to another realm, or was it just an elaborate trinket with no real significance?

Aria's doubts were put to the test one evening when, as she lay in bed, the room seemed to be enveloped in an otherworldly glow. The symbols on the pendant pulsed with an eerie light, casting intricate patterns on the walls. Aria's heart raced, a mixture of fear and fascination coursing through her veins.

Then, in the midst of the shimmering light, a figure appeared. It was a man, dressed in robes that seemed to be made of pure light. His eyes held a depth of wisdom and kindness, and his presence exuded a sense of peace that Aria had never felt before. The man spoke, his voice a gentle melody that seemed to resonate within her very soul.

"Do not be afraid, Aria," he said, his words carrying a weight of assurance. "The pendant you hold is a key—a key to the spiritual realm that exists beyond what your eyes can see. I am here to guide you, to help you navigate this hidden world and uncover the truths that have remained veiled."

Aria's heart raced as she listened to the man's words. She was torn between awe and disbelief. Could this truly be happening? Was she standing on the threshold of a reality she had never imagined? She wanted to believe, to embrace this new adventure, but her logical mind held her back.

The man seemed to understand her inner turmoil. "Your doubts are natural," he said, his voice filled with understanding. "But remember, faith is not the absence of doubt; it is the willingness to believe in something greater than yourself. Just as you have found solace in the unseen truths of God's love, so too can you explore the mysteries of this hidden realm."

As he spoke, the man extended his hand, offering the pendant back to Aria. With a mixture of trepidation and curiosity, Aria accepted it. The moment her fingers closed around the pendant, she felt a surge of energy—a connection to something beyond the tangible world. The room around her seemed to shift, the boundaries between reality and the unknown blurring.

"You are not alone in this journey," the man continued. "I will be your mentor, your guide, as you navigate the realms of angels and demons. Together, we will unveil truths that have remained hidden, and you will come to understand the intricacies of the spiritual battles that shape the world around you."

Aria looked into the man's eyes, a whirlwind of emotions stirring within her. Skepticism warred with fascination, fear with excitement.

She had always yearned for something greater than the ordinary, something that would give her life purpose and meaning. Could this hidden world be the answer she had been searching for?

As if sensing her thoughts, the man smiled—a smile that held a promise of adventure, growth, and transformation. "The journey ahead will not be easy," he said. "But remember, just as you have found strength in your faith, so too will you find strength in the knowledge that you are not alone. You have been chosen for a purpose, Aria, and you possess a power that can shape the destiny of both realms."

With those words, the room seemed to return to its normal state. The man's presence faded, leaving Aria in a state of wonder and uncertainty. She looked down at the pendant in her hand, the symbols shimmering as if to reaffirm the reality of the encounter.

The pendant became a captivating enigma, its secrets intertwined with Aria's daily life. She found herself drawn to its presence, her fingers tracing the intricate patterns whenever her thoughts wandered. The symbols seemed to hold a language of their own, a language that whispered of mysteries waiting to be unraveled.

The mentor's visits became more frequent, each encounter deepening Aria's curiosity and expanding her understanding of the hidden realms. He shared stories of ancient battles between angels and demons, of cosmic forces that shaped the destinies of both humans and supernatural beings.

With every tale, Aria's skepticism began to wane, replaced by a growing awareness of the profound truths that lay just beyond the veil of reality.

Their interactions were like glimpses into a world that existed parallel to her own—a world where celestial beings battled for the souls of humanity, where choices had far-reaching consequences beyond the physical realm. Aria learned about the intricacies of spiritual warfare, the battles that raged in the unseen dimensions, and the role humans played in the cosmic tapestry.

One evening, as they sat in the glow of a flickering candle, the mentor spoke of the importance of discernment. "Aria," he said, his voice carrying a weight of wisdom, "just as you navigate the complexities of human relationships and emotions, so too must you learn to discern the intentions and influences of the spiritual forces around you. The battles you face extend beyond the surface, and your choices have an impact that resonates throughout eternity."

Aria listened intently, her heart and mind captivated by the mentor's words. She realized that her journey of faith and healing had prepared her for this new chapter, for the revelation of a reality that was both extraordinary and deeply intertwined with her own. The doubts that had once clouded her mind seemed to dissipate as she embraced the idea that there was more to life than met the eye.

With each interaction, Aria's bond with the mentor grew stronger. He became a source of guidance and wisdom, a steady presence in the midst of her uncertainty. He encouraged her to ask questions, to explore the depths of her curiosity, and to trust in the power of faith even in the face of the unknown.

As Aria delved deeper into the mysteries of the hidden realms, she began to notice subtle shifts in her perception of the world around her. The ordinary became tinged with the extraordinary—the rustle of leaves carried whispers of unseen beings, the glint of stars held the promise of cosmic battles, and the kindness of strangers felt like the touch of celestial hands.

The mentor's teachings were interwoven with passages from the Bible, connecting the ancient truths of Scripture with the revelations of the hidden realms. Aria found comfort in the familiarity of the verses, seeing them in a new light that illuminated the intersections between the spiritual and the earthly.

One day, the mentor shared a verse that resonated deeply with Aria's journey: "For we do not wrestle against flesh and blood, but against the rulers, against the authorities, against the cosmic powers over this present darkness, against the spiritual forces of evil in the heavenly places." (Ephesians 6:12, ESV)

As Aria pondered these words, she realized the significance of her role in the battles that were waged beyond human sight. She was not merely a bystander in this cosmic conflict; she was a warrior, armed with faith and the power to make choices that could impact the balance between light and darkness.

With every revelation, every interaction, Aria's skepticism transformed into a deep sense of purpose. The pendant that had once seemed like an ordinary artifact now represented a doorway to a world of wonder and responsibility. The mentor's presence was a reminder that she was never alone, that even in the midst of uncertainty, she had a guide who believed in her potential to shape the destiny of both realms.

As Aria continued to explore the hidden realms, she embarked on a journey of growth, courage, and transformation. The boundaries of her reality expanded, and she found herself embracing a destiny she had never imagined—one that intertwined her human experiences with the cosmic battles of angels and demons. Each step forward was a step deeper into the unknown, a step closer to understanding the mysteries that had been veiled for so long.

CHAPTER 5

Temptation and Struggle

Aria's journey of faith had taken root in her heart, bringing her closer to God with each passing day. She immersed herself in the Bible, finding solace and guidance within its pages. As she read stories of miracles and divine interventions, her belief in the power of the unseen grew stronger. Yet, amidst her quest for spiritual enlightenment, a new curiosity emerged—one that would lead her down a path she had never imagined.

One evening, while reading the book of Exodus, Aria came across a passage that piqued her interest. It was the story of Pharaoh's magicians who were able to replicate some of the miracles that Moses performed through their own mystical arts. The concept of magic and powerful abilities held an irresistible allure, and Aria found herself drawn to this account.

Intrigued by the idea that even those who practiced magic had abilities that could rival the supernatural, Aria delved deeper. She decided to read the entire book of Exodus to gain a broader understanding of the context in which these events unfolded. As she read about the plagues, the parting of the Red Sea, and the divine encounters, she felt a sense of awe and wonder. The story of the magicians, however, remained at the forefront of her thoughts.

Aria's fascination led her to further research, and she began to explore articles and videos online that discussed the role of magic and witchcraft in ancient times. During her search, she stumbled upon a video that spoke about a lesser-known book in the Bible—the book of Daniel. Intrigued, Aria clicked on the video and listened as the narrator recounted the story of Daniel and his encounter with Nebuchadnezzar's magicians, enchanters, and astrologers.

Intrigued by this new perspective, Aria decided to delve into the book of Daniel. She read about the dreams and interpretations, the miraculous deliverance from the lions' den, and the visions of future events. She found herself captivated by the narrative, especially the way in which Daniel's faith in God's wisdom triumphed over the perceived power of the enchanters and magicians.

One night, as Aria drifted into sleep, her mind was still filled with the stories she had read. In her dream, she found herself in a world that shimmered with magic—where she could change her appearance with a simple thought, where her movements were fluid and graceful, and where she felt a sense of power and confidence she had never experienced before. The dream was exhilarating, a glimpse into a reality where the limitations of her physical form were transcended.

Upon waking, Aria was left with a mixture of emotions. She marveled at the dream's vividness and the feelings it had evoked within her. She couldn't help but wonder if the dream was a reflection of the stories she had been reading—stories that hinted at the existence of abilities beyond the ordinary.

Driven by curiosity, Aria decided to return to the library. She was determined to explore the realm of magic and power from a different perspective. She found a book that delved into ancient practices and beliefs, including those related to witchcraft and mysticism. As she flipped through the pages, Aria's heart raced with a mixture of excitement and apprehension.

The book detailed various spells and rituals, each promising a connection to forces beyond the natural world. Aria's fingers traced the symbols and incantations, her heart a mix of wonder and doubt. She felt like an explorer in uncharted territory, standing at the crossroads of ancient knowledge and modern curiosity.

With a sense of caution, Aria began to experiment with simple spells—spells that promised to enhance her creativity and intuition. She spoke incantations softly under her breath, her heart beating with a mixture of anticipation and skepticism. To her surprise, she found herself experiencing moments of heightened awareness, as if the barriers between her and the unseen were temporarily lifted.

The ancient book, "Sorcery and Secrets: Unveiling the Mysteries of the Otherworld," had become Aria's gateway to a world of power beyond her imagination. Each whispered spell felt like a key to unlock a new realm of possibilities, and the allure of control over her life and the lives of others was intoxicating.

Aria's powers expanded beyond the individual level to affect events and circumstances. If she wanted to ace a test, she would cast a spell that seemed to channel knowledge directly into her mind. If she desired sunshine for a weekend outing, she'd weave a subtle incantation that gently nudged the weather's course. Her power was growing, and she reveled in its limitless potential.

Amidst her fascination with her newfound abilities, the mentor's visits became less frequent, his guidance seemingly unnecessary in the face of her growing prowess. She pushed his warnings aside, convinced that her control over the spells was infallible. She believed she was invincible, standing at the precipice of limitless power.

One evening, Aria stumbled upon a complex ritual in the ancient book. The words and symbols were intricate, promising power on a scale she had never imagined. With a mix of trepidation and excitement, she decided to cast the ritual, drawn by the allure of even greater influence and control.

The air crackled with energy as Aria followed the ritual's instructions, her heart pounding with a mixture of anticipation and uncertainty. The room seemed to vibrate with an otherworldly force, and the boundaries between reality and the supernatural began to blur. Aria's consciousness expanded, and for a brief moment, she glimpsed a realm beyond her senses—a realm inhabited by unseen entities.

As the ritual reached its climax, Aria felt a surge of power unlike anything she had experienced before. It was as if the very fabric of existence bent to her command. The forces she had summoned were at her disposal, their energies coursing through her veins like a river of possibilities. Aria's heart raced with exhilaration as she realized the depths of her capabilities.

Days turned into nights, and Aria's mastery over her powers grew. She cast spells that seemed to alter fate itself, manipulating circumstances to her advantage. Her influence reached beyond individuals, affecting the ebb and flow of events in her favor. The thrill of control was addictive, and she felt a growing sense of omnipotence.

Yet, as her power expanded, a hollowness settled within her. The connections she forged felt shallow, built on manipulation rather than genuine bonds. The mentor's warnings echoed faintly in her thoughts, like whispers of concern in a sea of triumph. But Aria's fascination with power drowned out the voice of reason.

One fateful night, Aria cast a spell in an attempt to help her mother. She believed that easing her mother's stress would protect her, shield her from the pain of her daughter's choices. With a mixture of determination and urgency, Aria chanted the incantation, her heart full of hope.

But this time, something went terribly wrong. The room trembled, shadows coiling like serpents around her. Aria's mother's health deteriorated rapidly, her condition becoming critical. Panic gripped Aria's heart as she realized the magnitude of her mistake. She had nearly killed her mother.

Tears streamed down Aria's face as she frantically tried to undo the spell. She cried out for help, for intervention, her voice a desperate plea to the unseen forces she had summoned. It was a battle against the very magic she had wielded, a battle that threatened to consume her.

In the midst of her desperation, the mentor materialized before her, his presence a beacon of hope in the chaos. Aria's eyes were red and swollen, her face streaked with tears. "Help me," she pleaded, her voice quivering with a mixture of fear and remorse. "I've made a terrible mistake. My mother... she's suffering because of me."

The mentor's gaze was a mix of empathy and determination. He stepped forward, his touch a comforting reassurance. "Aria, you're not alone in this," he said gently. "The darkness you've embraced led you astray, but there is a way out. It starts with acknowledging the path you've chosen."

Aria nodded, her heart heavy with guilt and fear. She realized that her unchecked pursuit of power had led her to this point—a point where her choices had nearly cost her mother's life. The mentor's guidance became her lifeline, a way to navigate the chaos she had unleashed.

With the mentor's assistance, Aria began the painstaking process of reversing the spell and banishing the malevolent forces that had been awakened. Each word she spoke, each gesture she made, was imbued with a renewed sense of purpose—a purpose that stemmed from her determination to make amends.

As the darkness waned, Aria felt exhaustion wash over her, mingling with relief. She sank into a chair, her body trembling with the weight of her actions. The mentor's presence remained unwavering, a source of comfort in the aftermath of the storm.

"I've seen the consequences of my choices," Aria admitted, her voice trembling with remorse. "I've seen the darkness I've allowed to consume me."

The mentor's gaze was filled with compassion as he nodded. "Acknowledging your mistakes is the first step toward redemption," he reassured her. "The path you've chosen is not one of light or authenticity. It's a path that leads to pain and isolation."

Aria's heart wavered between guilt and determination. She had glimpsed the darkness within her, the darkness that had nearly cost her mother's life. The mentor's words resonated within her, a glimmer of hope in the midst of her remorse.

"I can't afford to lose anyone else I love," she whispered, her voice choked with emotion. The mentor's presence radiated understanding, a silent affirmation that she was not alone in this battle.

"The journey to redemption begins with acknowledging your mistakes and choosing a different path," the mentor said gently. "I'll be here to guide you, Aria."

As Aria listened to his words, relief flooded through her—a relief she hadn't felt in a long time. She realized that the path she had been walking was treacherous, but she was no longer walking it alone. With the mentor's guidance and her newfound determination, Aria was ready to face the challenges ahead and reclaim the light that had once illuminated her heart.

CHAPTER 6

Persistent Prayer

Aria's world had spiraled into chaos, the consequences of her choices becoming all too real. As she stared into the abyss of her mistakes, she felt a burning desire to find a way out. The mentor's guidance had become her anchor, his presence a beacon of hope in the midst of her darkness.

With a heavy heart, Aria turned to prayer. Each night, she retreated to her room, her hands clasped in fervent supplication. She poured out her regrets, her fears, and her longing for forgiveness. Her tears mingled with her prayers, a desperate plea for intervention, for redemption.

Time passed, and Aria's prayers continued with unwavering persistence. She sought solace in the divine, clinging to a faith that had been tested by her own choices. The mentor had shown her the path, but it was her own journey to walk—a journey that required her to confront her mistakes and seek divine intervention.

Amidst her prayers, Aria began to sense a shift in the air—a presence that transcended the boundaries of her room. It was a presence that radiated compassion and understanding, a presence that she recognized from her earlier encounter. It was the presence of Jesus.

One night, as Aria knelt in prayer, her heart heavy with remorse, a soft, reassuring voice filled the room. "Aria," the voice whispered, carrying a warmth that eased her soul, "you are not alone. I am with you, even in your darkest moments."

Aria's eyes filled with tears as she felt a rush of comfort envelop her. The weight of her mistakes seemed to lift, replaced by a sense of forgiveness and hope. It was a reminder that even in her deepest struggles, there was a hand reaching out to guide her.

With each passing day, Aria's connection with Jesus grew stronger. She poured over the pages of the Bible, seeking solace in the stories of redemption and grace. She found herself drawn to the accounts of Jesus' miracles and teachings, each word resonating with her own journey of redemption.

One evening, as Aria read about Jesus' unwavering love and the power of his sacrifice, she realized that the darkness she had embraced was not insurmountable. She realized that the demons and the manipulation were not aligned with God's will —they were distortions of the light she had been seeking.

With a renewed sense of determination, Aria lifted her voice in prayer once again, this time not with desperation, but with a steadfast resolve. "Jesus," she prayed, her voice unwavering, "I want to break free from this darkness. I want to leave behind the path of manipulation and embrace your light."

As her prayer echoed in the stillness, Aria felt a presence surrounding her—a presence that radiated love and acceptance. It was a presence that whispered of forgiveness and second chances, a presence that carried the promise of rescue.

In that moment, a blinding light filled the room, and Aria felt a warm embrace that seemed to transcend the boundaries of the physical world. She felt a sense of purity wash over her, as if the darkness that had clouded her soul was being cleansed.

When the light subsided, Aria found herself standing in a place that was both familiar and new—a place of clarity and peace. Before her stood Jesus, his gaze unwavering and filled with compassion. "You have chosen the path of redemption," he said softly, his words a balm to her wounded heart.

Tears welled in Aria's eyes as she looked upon the face of her rescuer. "I want to leave behind the darkness I've embraced," she whispered, her voice filled with conviction.

Jesus smiled, his presence radiating assurance. "You have taken the first step, Aria. The journey ahead won't be easy, but you won't walk it alone."

As Aria embraced the reality of her rescue, a sense of liberation washed over her. She realized that the darkness she had embraced was not a reflection of her true identity, but a distortion of the light within her. With Jesus by her side, she knew that the journey to reclaim her authenticity, her faith, and her purpose had begun.

In the presence of her rescuer, Aria's heart swelled with gratitude. She had found the strength to confront her mistakes, to seek forgiveness, and to embrace the light that had been waiting for her all along. With the mentor's guidance and Jesus' unwavering love, she was ready to face whatever challenges lay ahead and to walk the path from shadows to purpose.

Aria's journey of persistent prayer led her to a revelation that would forever change her perspective. As she delved deeper into her relationship with Jesus, she began to understand that the mentor who had guided her all along was none other than the Holy Spirit—the divine presence that had been by her side since the beginning.

One evening, as Aria sat in her room, the truth began to dawn on her. The pieces of the puzzle fell into place, and she realized that the mentor's guidance had always been aligned with Jesus' teachings. It was as if a veil had been lifted, revealing the Holy Spirit's role as her silent companion, her steady guide in the midst of her trials.

Tears of gratitude welled in Aria's eyes as she whispered, "You've been with me all this time, haven't you? The Holy Spirit—the mentor who never abandoned me."

A gentle breeze swept through the room, carrying with it a sense of affirmation and love. In that moment, Aria felt a profound connection with the Holy Spirit—an understanding that transcended words. She realized that her journey of redemption had been guided by the divine wisdom and love of her silent mentor.

With this realization came a renewed sense of purpose. Aria knew that she was not alone in her struggle to leave behind the darkness that had ensnared her. The Holy Spirit's presence provided her with the strength and guidance she needed to overcome the challenges that lay ahead.

One day, as the morning sun painted the sky with hues of gold and pink, Aria found herself standing before her mother. The weight of her mistakes and the depth of her remorse hung heavy in the air. She knew that the time had come for a heartfelt confession, for an honest reckoning of her choices and their consequences.

Taking a deep breath, Aria looked into her mother's eyes and began to speak. "Mom," she said softly, her voice laced with vulnerability, "there's something I need to tell you. I've made mistakes—choices that have hurt you and our relationship."

Her mother's gaze held a mixture of concern and compassion, her eyes mirroring the love she had always shown her daughter. "Aria, you can always talk to me," she responded gently, her voice an invitation for Aria to open up.

Tears welled in Aria's eyes as she continued. She shared the story of her journey into the darkness of manipulation, the spells she had cast, and the consequences that had nearly cost her mother's life. With each word, the weight on her heart began to lift, replaced by a sense of catharsis and release.

Her mother listened attentively, her expression a blend of understanding and empathy. When Aria's voice finally faltered, her mother stepped forward and embraced her tightly. "Aria," she said softly, her voice filled with love, "I forgive you. We all make mistakes, but what matters is how we choose to move forward."

Tears streamed down Aria's face as she clung to her mother, her heart overflowing with gratitude. The forgiveness she had received was a balm to her wounded soul, a reminder that redemption and reconciliation were possible even in the face of her darkest choices.

As Aria and her mother held each other, a sense of healing began to envelop them—a healing that went beyond words, mending the fractures that had formed between them. In that embrace, Aria realized the power of vulnerability and honesty —the power to rebuild what had been broken.

Amidst their embrace, Aria's mother spoke words that resonated deep within Aria's heart. "You know, Aria," she said gently, "there's a verse I've always found comforting. It's from Isaiah 43:18-19, and it goes like this: 'Forget the former things; do not dwell on the past. See, I am doing a new thing! Now it springs up; do you not perceive it? I am making a way in the wilderness and streams in the wasteland.'"

Aria's heart stirred as she listened to the words, a sense of hope blossoming within her. The verse felt like a promise of renewal and transformation—a promise that her mistakes did not define her, and that God was capable of bringing beauty from the ashes.

As the sun dipped below the horizon, Aria and her mother sat together, their hearts intertwined in a moment of profound connection. The Holy Spirit's presence was palpable, a gentle reminder that redemption was not just a possibility, but a reality that was unfolding before them.

In the days that followed, Aria continued to seek guidance from the Holy Spirit—the mentor who had been with her all along. With each step she took towards light and authenticity, she felt the Holy Spirit's guidance, a steady hand leading her through the challenges of her journey.

With a heart filled with gratitude, Aria knew that her rescue was a testament to the power of love, forgiveness, and the unwavering presence of the Holy Spirit. As she walked the path from shadows to purpose, she held onto the promise that she was never alone, that the best mentor she could have was the divine presence guiding her every step of the way.

CHAPTER 7

The Warrior

Aria's journey of redemption had transformed her from a lost soul into a warrior of light. It all began with an unexpected opportunity that opened the door for her to share her story and make a difference in the lives of those ensnared by darkness.

One day, Aria's friend Lily, who had been absent from her life for so long, unexpectedly reached out to her. Lily had heard about Aria's transformation and the journey she had undertaken to break free from the clutches of manipulation and witchcraft. Intrigued by Aria's story, Lily shared it with a group of individuals who were struggling with similar challenges. These were individuals caught in the web of deception, seeking a way out but not knowing where to turn.

Lily's act of reaching out was a significant turning point. She knew that Aria's story held the potential to inspire and bring hope to those who were desperately seeking answers. Lily's own absence from Aria's life had been a painful choice, but she believed that by connecting Aria with those who needed her message, she could play a role in healing wounds and mending relationships.

Lily had learned about Aria's battle with witchcraft through a mutual acquaintance who had attended one of Aria's speaking engagements. This acquaintance of Lily's had shared a link to a website belonging to a support group. On this website, a video was hosted, showcasing an interview with Aria in front of an engaged audience.

Lily had watched Aria's interview with a mix of pride and humility. Seeing her friend share her journey, her struggles, and her newfound strength on such a public platform had been both inspiring and humbling. The way Aria spoke about her experiences resonated with Lily on a profound level, and it reinforced her belief that Aria's story could indeed be a source of healing for many.

The truth was that Lily had been wrestling with her own internal struggles during the time she had distanced herself from Aria. Her heart had carried the weight of guilt and regret, knowing that her absence had hurt her friend deeply. Lily had been battling her own insecurities and doubts, fearing that she wasn't worthy of Aria's friendship and the light she brought into her life.

Deeply moved by Aria's story of redemption, Lily had felt a renewed connection to her friend. The realization that both of them had been on separate paths of growth and self-discovery had touched Lily's heart.

Aria's phone buzzed with a message from an unknown number —Lily's. The message simply read, "Aria, I think your story can help others. Would you be willing to share it?" Aria's heart swelled with a mix of surprise and gratitude. It was an invitation that she hadn't expected, an opportunity to use her journey as a beacon of hope for others.

With a resolute heart, Aria replied to Lily's message, expressing her willingness to share her story. She felt a sense of purpose welling up within her—a sense that her own pain and struggles could be transformed into a force for good.

The organizers of the community gathering soon learned about Aria's journey through Lily's connection. They recognized the importance of addressing the rise of witchcraft and manipulation, especially among young individuals seeking answers in the wrong places. They believed that Aria's story could shed light on the darkness that so many were grappling with.

Aria was approached with an invitation to speak at the event —an invitation she accepted without hesitation. She saw it as a chance to not only share her journey but to also extend a lifeline to those who felt trapped in the same web she had once been entangled in.

Stepping onto the stage that day, Aria's heart pounded with a mix of nerves and determination. She looked out at the audience, individuals whose faces held the weight of their struggles. The opportunity to speak was not just a chance to share her story—it was a chance to ignite a spark of hope in their hearts.

As Aria recounted her journey—from her own choices to her encounter with the Holy Spirit—the room was filled with a palpable sense of connection. She saw recognition in the eyes of her listeners, a recognition that mirrored her own experiences. With each word she spoke, Aria felt a bond forming, a bridge between her story and the stories of those who had come to listen.

By the time Aria concluded her speech, the room was filled with a silence that spoke volumes. It was a silence filled with the weight of her words, the impact of her journey. And then, one by one, individuals began to approach her with tears in their eyes and stories on their lips.

"I thought I was alone in this," a young man confessed, his voice cracking with emotion. "But hearing your story—it gives me hope that I can break free too."

Aria reached out and held his hand, her heart overflowing with empathy. "You're not alone," she reassured him. "There's a way out, and I'm here to walk that journey with you."

It was in that moment of connection that Aria realized she wasn't just sharing her story—she was leading others out of the darkness. She saw herself as a warrior of hope, a beacon of light that could guide others to the path of redemption.

Through moments of connection, unwavering confidence, and a growing understanding of her spiritual armor, Aria's conviction as a warrior solidified. She knew that her journey was a call to action, a call to be a vessel of God's light and love in a world that sometimes seemed shrouded in darkness.

Her journey wasn't without challenges. There were moments when doubt crept in, when the weight of the battles seemed overwhelming. But each time Aria felt uncertain, she turned to the Holy Spirit—the silent mentor who had guided her every step of the way. Through prayer and meditation, she found the strength to press on, to continue fighting the battles that mattered most.

As Aria embraced her role as a warrior, she felt a deep sense of purpose and fulfillment. She knew that her journey wasn't just about herself—it was a call to be a light-bearer, a truth-speaker, and a guide for those who needed to break free from the shadows. With the Holy Spirit as her guide and her armor, Aria was prepared to stand firm against the forces of darkness, ready to fight the battles that would ultimately lead to the triumph of light.

An unexpectedly beautiful thing began to happen within her friendship with Lily. They reconnected in a different way, bound by their shared interest in helping people break free from witchcraft and manipulation. Their conversations shifted from shallow gossip and idle activities to deep discussions about their purpose and their faith.

Aria and Lily realized that their friendship had been remolded by God into a purposeful companionship. Together, they became intercessors, praying earnestly for those seeking deliverance. Their journey had deepened their bond, revealing the beauty of a friendship rooted in a shared calling to praise God and fight against the darkness that threatened to consume lives.

With the Holy Spirit as their guide, Aria and Lily were on a new journey—one that focused on bringing light to the lives of others, healing wounds, and battling against the spiritual forces that sought to undermine God's plan. As they walked this path side by side, their friendship radiated a sense of purpose and strength that only came from aligning themselves with a higher calling.

With the Holy Spirit's guidance, Aria's transformation into a warrior was complete. Her journey was no longer just about her—it was about standing strong against the forces of darkness, bringing hope to those in need, and living a life that glorified God.

Aria and Lily embarked on a journey that was not only transformative but also incredibly powerful. As they continued to share Aria's story of redemption and liberation from manipulation and witchcraft, they encountered individuals with stories that resonated deeply. Their mission took them to community centers, churches, and gatherings where people shared their struggles, hopes, and aspirations.

At one of these gatherings, Aria and Lily were moved by the story of a young woman named Sophia. Sophia's eyes glistened with tears as she spoke about her past involvement in witchcraft. Her voice trembled as she recounted the desperate rituals she had performed, seeking power and acceptance. However, her journey took a dark turn when she realized that the power she had gained came at the cost of her own well-being and the well-being of others.

"I was lost," Sophia confessed, her voice quivering. "I thought I had control, but it was controlling me. I was hurting people, and I was hurting myself. I didn't know how to escape the darkness I had fallen into."

Aria and Lily listened intently, their hearts heavy with empathy. They knew that Sophia's story was not unique—that there were countless individuals trapped in a similar cycle of manipulation and despair. But they also knew that their message of redemption, backed by Aria's own journey, could offer a glimmer of hope to those like Sophia.

As Aria stood before the gathered audience, she shared Sophia's story along with her own. She spoke about the power of breaking free from manipulation, the strength of faith, and the hope that comes from knowing that no one is beyond redemption. Her words resonated deeply, not just with Sophia, but with everyone present.

Their missions began to grow in scope and impact. Aria's story spread, and soon, she was invited to speak on a local Christian television show. It was an opportunity that held the potential to reach even more hearts, to bring light to those who were searching for answers.

On the day of the interview, Aria felt a mixture of excitement and nervousness. The studio lights were bright, and the cameras were rolling. As the host introduced her, Aria took a deep breath and began to speak. Her voice was steady, her words filled with conviction.

She spoke about her journey—from the depths of manipulation and darkness to the heights of redemption and light. She shared stories of individuals she had met along the way, stories of pain, struggle, and ultimately, transformation. Aria's authenticity and unwavering faith shown through as she shared the message of hope that had become the cornerstone of her journey.

The response was overwhelming. Aria's message resonated with viewers, and her story struck a chord with those who had been silently battling their own struggles. The outpouring of support and encouragement was immense, and Aria's journey began to gain recognition beyond what she had anticipated.

Her newfound fame, however, was not about personal glory. Aria remained steadfast in her commitment to the message of redemption and the power of faith. She continued to partner with Lily, reaching out to individuals who sought deliverance from darkness and manipulation. Their journey had become more than a mission—it had become a movement, a force for good that was breaking chains and offering hope.

Through Aria's appearances on television and Lily's steadfast support, they were able to extend their reach even further. The impact they had on the lives of countless individuals was immeasurable, and their journey became a testament to the transformative power of faith, friendship, and the unwavering guidance of the Holy Spirit.

As Aria reflected on her journey, she realized that her journey from shadows to light had been a call to action, a call to be a warrior of hope and a vessel of God's love. And as she stood side by side with Lily, she knew that their friendship, once rekindled, had been molded by God into a purposeful companionship—one that sought to praise God, fight darkness, and bring light to the lives of those who needed it most.

Amid the whirlwind of interviews, appearances, and speaking engagements, Aria received an email that brought a mixture of shock and anticipation. The subject line read, "From a Heart Seeking Forgiveness." It was an email from an unfamiliar sender, and as Aria opened it, her heart raced with a mix of emotions.

The words on the screen were from her father, the man who had left her life when she was just a child. His message was heartfelt, filled with regret and remorse. He spoke of the pain he had caused, the mistakes he had made, and the years he had lost. He acknowledged the hurt he had inflicted on Aria and her mother and expressed a deep desire for forgiveness.

Aria's eyes welled up with tears as she read her father's words. It was a moment she had never imagined—her father reaching out to her after years of absence. She could feel the weight of his regret, the sincerity of his apology. As she read his email, she saw a different side of her father, a side that she had never truly known.

She shared the email with her mother, and together, they sat down to discuss their feelings. Aria's mother, who had always been a pillar of strength, listened to Aria's thoughts and emotions with understanding. She spoke of the importance of forgiveness, not just for her father's sake, but for Aria's own healing.

"You have the power to break free from the pain of the past," her mother said gently. "Forgiveness doesn't excuse what happened, but it frees you from carrying the burden of resentment."

With her mother's support, Aria took a deep breath and composed a reply to her father's email. Her words were honest and vulnerable, expressing her own journey of healing and growth. She acknowledged the pain she had felt, the years of longing, and the complexities of their relationship.

But amidst her words of hurt, Aria found the strength to extend forgiveness. She realized that forgiveness was not just a gift for her father—it was a gift for herself. It was a step towards healing, a way to let go of the bitterness that had held her captive for so long.

As Aria hit the send button, a sense of relief washed over her. She had taken a step towards reconciliation, towards rebuilding a connection that had been fractured. Her father's email had opened a door—one that led to the possibility of rebuilding a relationship that had been lost for years.

Days turned into weeks, and Aria's father responded to her email with gratitude and humility. He acknowledged the pain he had caused and expressed his deep regret for the years he had missed. He didn't make excuses; instead, he accepted responsibility for his actions.

In one of his emails, he wrote, "I understand if forgiveness takes time, if it's a journey you need to take at your own pace. But know that I am committed to being a better father, a presence in your life."

Aria's heart softened as she read his words. She could sense the sincerity in his tone, the genuine desire for reconciliation. With each exchange of emails, their conversations grew more open, more vulnerable. Aria found herself sharing her own journey, her transformation from darkness to light, and the faith that had become her guiding force.

Through these exchanges, Aria realized that her father was also on a journey of growth and change. He had reached out not to erase the past, but to build a new foundation for their relationship—a foundation rooted in understanding, forgiveness, and a shared commitment to healing.

As Aria continued to correspond with her father, her mother's unwavering support became a source of strength. Her mother encouraged her to take each step with wisdom and grace, reminding her that forgiveness was a process, not a one-time decision.

Her story had become a testament to the transformative power of God's love—a love that could mend broken relationships, heal deep wounds, and guide souls from darkness to light.

CHAPTER 8

From Shadows to Light

Aria's journey had taken her from the depths of darkness to the heights of redemption. As she looked back on the path she had walked, she couldn't help but marvel at the transformation that had taken place within her. The once broken and confused girl had grown into a beacon of light—a warrior whose strength came not from her own abilities, but from her unshakable faith in God.

In the months that followed her reconciliation with her father, Aria's growth was evident to all who knew her. Her relationship with him continued to mend, slowly but surely. They shared stories, laughed, and rediscovered the joy of being in each other's lives. It wasn't without its challenges, but their commitment to healing was unwavering.

Aria's faith had deepened in ways she had never imagined. Her encounters with the Holy Spirit had not only transformed her, but they had also given her a powerful purpose. She had experienced the warmth of God's love, the guidance of His presence, and the reassurance that she was never alone. This faith was no longer just a part of her story—it was the foundation on which she stood.

With Lily by her side, Aria continued her mission to help those who were trapped in darkness. They reached out to individuals struggling with manipulation, addiction, and despair, offering not just words of comfort, but genuine understanding and hope.

One day, as Aria sat in her room, reflecting on her journey, a thought crossed her mind—a thought that felt like a whisper from the Holy Spirit. She knew that her story was meant to be shared beyond the confines of her own experiences. She decided to write a book, a book that would chronicle her journey from shadows to light—a journey that was emblematic of the battles we all face.

As Aria penned her story, she poured her heart and soul onto the pages. She wanted her journey to serve as a reminder that no darkness is too deep to be penetrated by God's light. The process of writing became a cathartic experience, allowing her to revisit the pain of her past while embracing the promise of her future.

The book resonated with readers far and wide. Aria's honesty, vulnerability, and unwavering faith struck a chord with those who had walked similar paths. The messages of hope and redemption found their way into the hearts of those who needed them most, reminding them that they were not alone in their struggles.

With the success of her book, Aria was invited to speak at conferences, workshops, and events. Her story was a testament to the power of faith and the ability to overcome even the darkest of circumstances. Her presence on stage was magnetic—her words were a soothing balm to wounded hearts, a spark of inspiration to those seeking a way out.

Her journey had not only changed her life, but it had also changed the lives of countless others. Aria had become an example of resilience, forgiveness, and the transformative power of God's love. She knew that her story was not just about her—it was about the promise of a better future for all who dared to believe.

As Aria's influence continued to grow, she remained rooted in her faith, grounded by the guiding presence of the Holy Spirit. She lived out the Christian values she had embraced—compassion, forgiveness, and the unwavering commitment to being a light in the world. Her journey had become a living testimony to the promise that even the most shattered lives can be pieced back together by the hands of a loving God.

The book's closing pages held a message of hope, a message that Aria hoped would resonate with readers long after they had turned the final page:

"Dear friend, your journey is not defined by the shadows you've walked through. It's defined by the light that shines within you—a light that can dispel even the darkest of fears. Just as I found my way from shadows to light, you too can find your path of redemption and healing. Trust in the power of faith, the strength of love, and the promise of a better tomorrow."

And so, Aria's story came full circle—a journey that began in pain and darkness had blossomed into a triumphant testament of faith, forgiveness, and the indomitable strength of the human spirit. Through her experiences, she had learned that even the most shattered hearts could be made whole again, and that God's light could shine even in the deepest of shadows.

In the midst of her journey, Aria had an unexpected encounter—one that held the promise of even more healing and reconciliation. Aria's father had remarried and started a new family, and she had half-siblings from this new union. Despite the years of separation, Aria's heart remained open to the possibility of building relationships with them.

One day, as Aria was preparing for a book signing event, she noticed a group of individuals standing in the crowd. As she looked closer, she realized that they were her half-siblings—her father's children from his second marriage. Her heart skipped a beat, and a mix of emotions surged within her.

With a warm smile, they approached Aria, their eyes shining with excitement. Introductions were exchanged, and the awkwardness that often accompanies such meetings quickly dissolved. Aria was met with genuine warmth and acceptance, and she could see the shared connection that bound them together as a family.

As they chatted, Aria learned that her half-siblings were Christians as well. Their faith had been nurtured by their parents, and they had grown up hearing stories about their older sister, Aria.

They had followed her journey of transformation, and their hearts were filled with pride for the woman she had become.

"We've always looked up to you," one of her half-sisters said with a smile. "Your story inspired us to believe that God can truly turn darkness into light."

Tears welled up in Aria's eyes as she hugged each of them. The bitterness of the past seemed to melt away, replaced by the warmth of newfound connection and understanding. Her journey had led to the healing and restoration of relationships that had been fractured by circumstance.

The book signing event became a special moment of celebration—a celebration of Aria's journey, her newfound family ties, and the power of faith to bridge gaps that seemed insurmountable. Aria's half-siblings expressed their admiration for her courage and resilience, and Aria felt a sense of gratitude that words couldn't fully express.

"We've prayed for this day," one of her half-brothers shared. "To finally meet you, to be a part of your journey."

In that moment, Aria felt a profound sense of unity—a unity that transcended differences, misunderstandings, and the passage of time. She realized that her journey was intertwined with theirs, that her story was now a part of their collective narrative.

As the event concluded, Aria stood side by side with her half-siblings, a united front that symbolized the power of love, faith, and the promise of restoration. They posed for a photo together, their smiles radiating a sense of joy and connection.

The encounter with her half-siblings became another chapter in Aria's journey—a chapter of unexpected blessings and renewed relationships. The wounds of the past had been replaced with a renewed sense of purpose, a purpose that extended beyond her own life and touched the lives of those she now called family.

In the years that followed, Aria's influence continued to grow, her impact extending far beyond what she could have ever imagined. Her story reached corners of the world she had never visited, inspiring countless individuals to find hope in the midst of darkness. Her journey, once marked by pain and confusion, had become a beacon of light that guided others toward the path of redemption.

As Aria looked back on her story, she marveled at the way God had taken her from shadows to light. She had emerged from her struggles not just as a survivor, but as a conqueror—a conqueror who wielded the weapon of faith against the forces of darkness. And in the end, Aria's journey wasn't just about her—it was a testament to the promise that God's love can heal even the deepest of wounds, and that His light can shine through even the darkest of nights.

With a heart full of gratitude, Aria continued to live out her purpose, knowing that her story was a part of a greater narrative—a narrative of faith, forgiveness, and the triumphant power of God's love. And as she faced the future with hope and conviction, she held onto the truth that her journey, from shadows to light, was a testament to the promise of a better tomorrow.

The End.

Dear Readers,

As I reflect on the journey that Aria Everwood embarked upon, from the shadows of pain and manipulation to the brilliant light of faith and redemption, I am humbled by the power of stories. Our lives are a tapestry of experiences—some woven with joy, others with pain—but all contributing to the intricate design of who we are.

In sharing Aria's story with you, my hope was not only to offer a tale of transformation but to remind us all that no darkness is too deep for God's light to penetrate. We are all warriors on a battlefield, fighting battles that often remain unseen. Yet, just as Aria discovered, we are not alone in our struggles. Our faith, our friendships, and the guiding hand of the Holy Spirit can lead us from despair to triumph.

I want to extend my heartfelt gratitude to each of you for joining Aria on her journey. Your support, your engagement, and your willingness to open your hearts to this story have touched me deeply. I believe that every story has the power to touch a life, to inspire change, and to kindle hope—and your embrace of Aria's journey has reaffirmed that belief.
In closing, I am reminded of the words found in Psalm 139:11-12 (NIV):

"If I say, 'Surely the darkness will hide me and the light become night around me,' even the darkness will not be dark to you; the night will shine like the day, for darkness is as light to you."

May these words resonate with you, reminding you that no matter how deep the darkness may seem, God's light is ever-present, ready to lead us back to the path of hope, healing, and redemption.

With gratitude,
Jayne Adriel

Made in the USA
Monee, IL
18 December 2023

49492188R00039